A Swift Ad

Laurella Swift and the Keys of Time

Allison Parkinson

A Tiger's Eye Book
<u>www.tigerseyebooks.co.uk</u>

I

Laurella Swift and the Keys of Time

Published by Tiger's Eye Books
www.tigerseyebooks.co.uk

Illustrations: Allison Parkinson
Design: Stephen Shillito

First paperback print edition:
2021 in the United Kingdom

ISBN: 978-1-9161948-2-3

For Ella and Laura

IV

Chapter 1

Laurella Swift pushed open the door of the Freshwater Heart Trust shop and heard the familiar tinkle of the old brass bell.

"Hi Joy," she called as her parents followed her into the charity shop.

An elderly, slightly portly black lady, immaculately dressed in a white and purple floral dress with matching lilac cardigan and court shoes, rushed around the counter and hugged all three, in turn, reserving an extra-long, almost suffocating bear hug for Laurella. The 10-year-old was instantly enveloped in the pensioner's familiar rose perfume – a delicate and uplifting aroma that seemed to epitomise Joy.

"Look how she's grown; what a fine young lady!" exclaimed Joy in her warm, Bajan accent. "And such a pretty outfit too – come now darlin', give us a twirl."

Laurella obliged with an effortless pivot. As she spun, some of her beaded braids took fight momentarily before coming back to rest on the

1

shoulders of her biker style leather jacket. It had taken her mum hours to section and plait her dark brown curls, but the effect was stunning.

There was no doubting it; mixed race hair did demand a lot of time and effort. And although Laurella sometimes wished she could just gather her hair into a silky ponytail in seconds, just like her friends with straight hair could, she liked her curls and their versatility.

"So, when did you arrive," asked Joy, putting on her spectacles to take a closer look at the sparkly butterfly motif on her 'honorary' granddaughter's top.

"Yesterday afternoon," replied Laurella's mum. "And do you know, Joy, I could literally feel myself unwinding as soon as we drove off the ferry."

Laurella caught her dad's eye and they both smirked. Her mum said the same thing each and every time they holidayed on the Isle of Wight.

"So, tell me, girl, what's been happening since I saw you last?" said Joy. "Mummy and Daddy, you go browse around the shop for bargains, me and liccle Laurella here have got some serious catching up to do."

Laurella hadn't called her parents mummy and daddy since Year One. She'd flinch if anyone said the same thing to her back in Catford, but she didn't

2

mind when Joy said it. It was a West Indian 'thing' and it sounded so warm and loving.

Laurella took out her smartphone and began to show Joy what she'd been up to since starting Year Five. She was halfway through the story of her school trip to the British Museum when her mum interrupted her to show them both a large red rug with tassels at either end. It was decorated with stylised symmetrical leaves, flowers and branches, which were picked out in vibrant blues, oranges and yellows.

"Look what I've just found, Laurella. It'd be perfect for your bedroom. Do you like it?" asked her mum, offering the rug to her for closer inspection.

Laurella's mouth suddenly flooded with saliva. She swallowed uncomfortably and noticed that her mum's voice had started to echo in her ears. Her stomach lurched as if she was on a small boat being tossed by huge waves and when she closed her eyes, she felt herself slowly spiralling as if being sucked into a whirlpool. Laurella snapped her eyes back open and the spinning stopped.

"Are you OK love?" asked her mum, quickly taking the rug back and placing her hand on her daughter's forehead. "You've gone really pale."

"It's very stuffy in here today," Joy quickly interjected. "Why don't you leave the rug on the

3

counter for safekeeping and I'll take Laurella outside for a bit of fresh air? She'll be right in no time, don't fret darlin'."

"Are you sure?" asked her mum, turning from Joy to her daughter. "We can go if you like and come back later when you're feeling better?"

The echoing had stopped now, and the feeling of nausea was subsiding. "I'm fine mum, honestly," said Laurella. "But I don't really fancy going shopping at the moment. Can't you and dad have a look around the other charity shops while I stay here with Joy?"

"It's no problem," smiled Joy. "I'll be glad of the company."

"Well as long as you don't mind," said her mum.

"Not more shopping," groaned Laurella's dad, winking back at his daughter, as he playfully marched her mum over the threshold. Her parents loved mooching around charity shops. It was their guilty pleasure.

"Come, sweetheart, let's get some fresh air too," beamed Joy, taking Laurella's arm and leading her to the door.

As they stepped out into the breaking late spring sunshine Joy turned to Laurella with a look of urgency and excitement. "I've got something very important to tell you darlin' – and it's going to change your life forever!"

4

Chapter 2

The pensioner led Laurella to a sun-bleached garden table for sale outside the shop, pulled out a chair and gently gestured for her to sit. Joy grabbed another chair and pulled it close to her.

"You know I love you like my own and I would never tell you no lie don't you girl? Well, I'm going to tell you something now that is so fantastical, you're going to think I've lost my marbles.

"I know you've had that sicky, sicky feeling in the shop before and it's got nothing to do with dodgy lightbulbs or stuffy rooms. I know this for sure because I get it too – and it's only ever in this shop, isn't it? And it happens when you go near certain things like that rug just now, doesn't it?"

Without waiting for a response Joy continued excitedly: "You and I have got a very special gift. There may be millions of others like us or we may be the only ones in the whole world with this gift but all I know for certain is that, here and now, it's only us two.

"Some of the items donated to this shop are old,

very old and I don't know how, and I don't know why but some of them seem to still be connected to those earlier times – like they're aerials picking up live transmissions from the past. No-one else seems to be able to sense these transmissions as we can. But we can do much more than that girl – we can step right into the past!"

Laurella's mind began to whirl like a typhoon.

"Let me get this right, Joy," said Laurella, slowly and carefully choosing her words. "Are you telling me that you and I have the power to travel back in time – to the past – and see people that lived and died hundreds or thousands of years ago?"

"Not travel back, exactly, because what we consider to be the past may still be the present in another dimension," replied the pensioner but she stopped talking when she saw Laurella's mouth gape open.

"Look, "continued Joy after a few moments. "Imagine time like a large house with many, many rooms. You could be in one room, happily living your life in the present and in another room, Cleopatra may be happily living hers in parallel to yours. Usually, your lives will never, ever cross because the walls of the rooms keep you apart. But if there is a door between some of the rooms and you hold the 'key' to some of those doors, like that red rug or something else from the shop, you can go from room to room and meet Cleopatra.

"Are you telling me you've met Cleopatra?" exclaimed Laurella.

"No, no child," laughed Joy. "Well, at least not yet. But I have been to what we call Ancient Egypt. It was a plastic fridge magnet which had a fragment of ancient papyrus glued to the centre of it that turned out to be my key for that trip. That's how it seems to work. It doesn't have to be the whole item, you see, just the tiniest particle from another time can act as an aerial.

"I've met some amazing people from many different times and many different places – all because of this shop and some of the special things in it. It only seems to happen in the shop too – like it's a giant amplifier turning up the frequency of the transmissions. But when the things leave the shop, they're not keys any more, they're just ordinary items."

"But how can people who died ages ago still be alive? No-one can live for thousands of years; we both know that," protested Laurella, glancing down at Joy's worn wedding band.

"I can't give you all of the answers, darlin' because I'm still struggling to get my head around all of this too," said Joy. "Of course, we all die but we might just die in one dimension but still remain alive in others. Try to imagine that house again; you could be living one life in one room whilst also living slightly different versions of your life in another room, or ten rooms, or hundreds of rooms or even thousands of rooms!

"It's all got to do with atoms, I think. I read somewhere that everything in the universe, including me and you, the clothes we wear, the food we eat, the homes we live in, the ground we stand on and the air we breathe is all made up of tiny atoms. And atoms can't die, you see, they just turn into something else. So maybe we're like an ever-lasting pile of building blocks that are being constantly broken down and then rebuilt into the next model."

Rather than calming Laurella, each explanation offered by Joy simply whipped up another anxious surge of questions.

"How do you get to these places and how do you know you're going to be safe?" Laurella asked, starting to feel quite frightened. "When people realise you're not from their time they might want to hurt you – or even kill you. They might think you're a witch!"

Joy leaned closer, gently took hold of Laurella's hands, and looked directly into the girl's wide, chestnut eyes. "If I'm really honest I can't be 100 per cent sure darlin'," she answered.

"All I can go on is my own experience. I've been travelling for years now and although I've had some pretty hairy moments I've never got hurt. When people ask questions, I just tell them that I come from a different place to them, which is true. But every journey seems to be for a reason. Once I've figured out the reason and done what I need to do it's always time for me to come back home, safely."

"But how do you get there?" persisted Laurella. "And how do you explain where you've been. People must miss you and wonder where you are."

"That's the remarkable thing about it," said Joy. "I might spend days in those other places but when I come back not even a second's gone by. Time seems to work very differently in other dimensions you see. Don't ask me how or why this can all happen – I'm not a scientist but I think it might have something to do with quantum physics. I read something on the internet once about parallel universes or some such, but it never said anything about crossing dimensions through a charity shop!

"And getting there and back is easy, peasy. Your key will tell you when it's time to go by giving you that sicky, sicky feeling. But you don't have to worry. You just have to relax, stay close to your key and put up with that nasty feeling for just a few seconds. It soon passes and then you get the most amazing sensation like you're riding a rollercoaster inside a kaleidoscope."

Laurella liked the sound of that. She loved rollercoasters and any other sort of scary adrenaline ride. But just like the unexpected jolts you get while riding on a ghost train, Laurella suddenly remembered her mum and dad. They still grabbed hold of her hand when crossing a busy road – it was so embarrassing. They'd go mad if they found out she was crossing into other dimensions to who knows where – or when.

"I don't like keeping secrets from mum and dad but I'm frightened that if I tell them what you've just told me they'll think we've both gone mad," Laurella said anxiously.

"I know that darlin', I would never ask you to lie to your parents or keep anything from them. But sometimes when you grow up you do lose a bit of the wonder and belief in magic that you have as a child," said Joy sadly. "If you want to tell them you must do so, and I'll back you all the way. They might not believe us, and they might decide that it would be better if we don't see each other anymore but I'd rather take that risk than never tell you what I know to be the truth – however crazy it may seem."

Laurella fell silent, contemplating the potential

consequences of Joy's words. She gazed down to the pavement and started to trace out random shapes with the toe of her high-top trainer as if trying to discover a mathematical solution to the problem in hand. Eventually, she looked up and let out a decisive sigh.

"Mum and dad know you too well to ever think that you would lie to me," she said. "Although they're adults I don't think their minds are as closed as some people's are. Dad's always saying that there are lots of things that we don't yet fully understand. Just because we haven't got an explanation for them doesn't mean that they don't exist. And as for mum – well she still sees magic everywhere. In fact, dad's always joking that she's away with the fairies. Even so, time travel through their favourite charity shop might be something that even they will still struggle to get their heads around so let's keep it to ourselves for now."

Joy beamed and allowed herself to relax at last. "So, there you have it," she said. "I've told you what I know, and I really thank you darlin' for believing me – you don't know how much that means to me. If you like we can go back inside now, you keep your distance from the rug until it's out of the shop and, if you don't want to tell your parents, we need never say any more about this conversation."

12

Laurella looked up at the slowly dispersing clouds and watched a gull glide towards an ever-expanding patch of blue. Her entire body tingled with a mixture of gut-wrenching fear and excitement as if she were on a rollercoaster, seconds away from careering down the first terrifying incline.

"Thanks, Joy," she said, taking in a deep breath. "But I quite fancy seeing what's behind the doors. Will you show me how?"

"That's my girl!" said Joy and the two friends celebrated with a triumphant high five.

Chapter 3

Laurella rubbed her now clammy palms down her black leggings and glanced nervously over at the rug.

"Can you come with me Joy?" she asked anxiously.

"I can't sweetheart, because I don't think we pick up the same transmissions," Joy explained. "That rug is your key to a particular door, but I don't think the door will open for me. The keys choose us rather than the other way round, you see.

"But remember, you don't have to go through the door. You always have a choice. We can just have a nice chat here until your parents come back if you like?"

It made far more sense to do just that rather than dive head-first and alone into an unknown time and place but Laurella could never resist a challenge.

Taking a deep breath, she smiled bravely at the pensioner and stepped towards the rug. She looked up fleetingly at the shop's gently ticking wall clock and noticed it was seven minutes past eleven.

Shivery waves of nausea began to rise within Laurella and then grow more turbulent with every tentative step towards the rug. As she got closer, she noticed that some of the yellow threads were beginning to glow.

"Don't fight it darlin', just relax and open your eyes. The sicky, sicky feeling will soon pass," said Joy. Her voice already sounded far away and echoing.

Gathering all her courage Laurella cautiously opened her eyes and saw the rails and shelves of the charity shop slowly turn at right angles and then suddenly splinter into a frieze of multi-coloured hexagons. Before she could fully register the beauty of the honeycomb the shapes and colours changed again; now they were violet stars, crimson diamonds, turquoise triangles, amber circles and magenta hearts. All flowing in symmetry like living stained glass, each intricate pattern more exquisite and hypnotising than the last. Her body seemed to be gliding in effortless waves; up and down, up and down — a calming, rhythmic sensation like the roll and pull of the tide or the gentle inhale and exhale of breath. All traces of nausea had vanished and had now been replaced with an overwhelming sense of euphoria.

Ever so gradually the waves subsided and Laurella became still. She watched passively as the shapes and colours around her slowly melted back into her new surroundings. Strange sounds and the heady smell of jasmine and sun-drenched herbs began to drift towards her and grew steadily louder and stronger. She focused and found herself standing on a highly polished marble floor in an enormous square hall, richly decorated with painted ceilings and filled with terracotta pillars, the size of redwood trees. At the top of each column crouched fabulously carved lions and white bulls with golden horns. Their wide, lifelike eyes glared ferociously down at her.

OK then, Laurella thought to herself, scanning her strange surroundings. *This definitely isn't Freshwater. But more to the point, where am I? And when?*

Laurella darted behind one of the huge stone pillars, nearest the edge of the palatial hall, hoping that it would keep her out of sight long enough for her to formulate some sort of plan of action.

She heard a faint fizzing sound behind her, like the crackle of static electricity. Turning around, she saw a large piece of square cloth, suspended from a golden rod, fixed horizontally to the wall. It had a red background and, in the centre, embroidered in shimmering gold thread, was a spectacular golden eagle with wings and talons outstretched. Some of the threads were glowing, just like the yellow threads in the old charity shop rug.

So, it's the threads that are my key, Laurella deduced. *At some point, they must have been unpicked from this cloth and woven into the rug.*

Buoyed up by her discovery, Laurella made a mental note of where the cloth hung in the hall on the west wall next to the seventh outer pillar – topped by a golden lion – then peered tentatively around the column. The cavernous, vaulted hall was packed with a multitude of adults of varied appearance and assorted dress, and as they spoke their voices combined to form an almost deafening hum. Some had dark skin like her dad, some were fair skinned like her mum and many had olive skin like hers. Some had straight hair; some had afro hair, but most had dark brown curls.

As far as she could see, all the men appeared to have manicured beards and moustaches and they wore an assortment of head-dresses including thick bands, bandanas, floppy caps and wrapped turbans.

A man stopped close to her pillar, completely blocking her view of the hall. He wore long, laced boots and an elaborately embroidered overcoat and stood so close to her that she could see each intricate stitch on the back of his coat. Laurella pressed herself into the pillar and willed her body to melt

17

into the stone.

Eventually, his footsteps trailed away and Laurella braved another peep. More people, men and women, had now entered the hall and were mingling with the other adults. The women wore flowing robes tied with tasselled belts and their long, dark curls were held back with golden combs. The men wore richly decorated belted robes with wide sleeves, beneath which flashed golden bangles. Thick golden hoops also hung from their ears and their tall, fluted hats looked like stiff fabric crowns.

Edging slightly forward for a closer look, Laurella noticed other men of similar dress standing silently around the perimeter who, to her alarm, held wicker shields, spears and large menacing daggers. Laurella darted back behind the pillar at the sight of the fearsome weapons. Wherever she was it looked pretty ancient. Was she in Troy or ancient Greece or had she stepped further back in time?

"What are you doing?" hissed a voice in her ear. The sudden noise made the hair bristle on the nape of her neck. She spun around to see an olive-skinned boy with short dark curls and piercing hazel eyes, staring into her face. He wore a long, red belted robe similar to the soldiers' gowns and by his side, fixing her with its amber eyes, stood a lion cub on a golden leash.

"I, I, I was just looking at all the people," Laurella stammered, her eyes darting from the cub's burning stare to his. *He's got a lion on a lead,* she exclaimed inwardly. *He's got a flippin' pet lion!*

Chapter 4

"Do you speak truthfully or are you here in the Hall of all Nations to do harm to your King, Cyrus the Great, King of Kings, King of Persia, King of Ashan, King of Medea, King of Babylon, King of Sumer and Akkad, King of the Four Corners of the World?" persisted the boy dramatically, his nose now just millimetres from hers.

"Yes, I swear I'm telling you the truth," protested Laurella, realising the enormity of being alone in strange surroundings and thousands of years from home. "I've only just arrived here and, to be perfectly honest, I can hardly believe my eyes!"

The boy maintained his unnerving stare for what felt like a lifetime and then slowly leaned back, puffed out his chest and, with an air of unashamed smugness, tilted his nose upwards. "Yes, I am satisfied that you indeed speak the truth, for I Artafarnah, son of Pantea and General Aryasb, brave warriors of the Achaemenid and Commanders of the Immortals, am an excellent judge of character," he declared.

The lion cub seemed to note the boy's more relaxed demeanour and sat down on its haunches, emitting a gravelly mew of agreement.

"You may remain here with me to watch this great spectacle," continued the boy, "for I too have never before attended our King's birthday feast."

Satisfied with the grandeur of his introduction and delighted to have the company of someone of his own age, the boy decided to dispense with further formality and allowed a wide, warm smile to light up his face.

"Zareen approves of you as well, don't you dearest?" he grinned, affectionately rubbing the cub behind her ear. Laurella longed to do the same and feel the cub's soft golden fur between her fingers but she didn't know if she should. Aside from all the probable complexities of ancient etiquette, the cute, oversized kitten already had a formidable set of fangs.

"So, tell me," he asked eagerly. "What is your name and where have you travelled from, for I do not recognise your regional dress?"

Laurella had to think quickly. The boy had mentioned Persia, the ancient name for Iran, so she couldn't say she was from London or even Londinium (the Roman name for London) because she was probably in a time well before the Roman

21

Empire. She hurriedly thought of the oldest name she could think of for England.

"I am Laurella," she declared formally. "I am a citizen of Catford in the kingdom of Albion. My home lies a very long way from here, so I am grateful to you for your hospitality."

"Cat-ford," repeated the boy, slowly rolling the word across his tongue as if he were tasting a new, strange flavour for the first time. "I have not heard of this city before. Is the cat sacred to your people? Do you worship the beast like the Egyptians worship the cat-headed effigies of their goddess Bastet?"

Laurella knew exactly what he was talking about. She'd seen a beautiful bronze figure of Bastet in cat form during her school trip to the British Museum. The museum also had huge granite statues of the goddess carved in the shape of a lion-headed woman.

"Not sacred exactly," explained Laurella. "But many people have cats as pets and consider them to be important members of their families." As she said the words, she found herself glancing down at the lion cub on a golden leash, still barely able to believe her eyes. "I think my town got its name from the large number of wild cats that used to live in the area a long time ago," she continued.

"We do have a statue of a cat," she smiled, thinking of the infamous black and white cat that

22

crouched above the sign for Catford Shopping Centre, ready to swipe unsuspecting shoppers with its huge fibreglass paw. "But we certainly don't worship it." The truth was many people detested the giant feline, considering it naff and tasteless, but she loved it.

"You also wear your hair in a manner that resembles the Egyptian style," remarked Artafarnah, looking at Laurella's beaded plaits. "But I have never seen this coloured ivory before."

"What these beads?" Laurella asked indignantly, pulling at one of her braids. She had nothing but contempt for the cruel 21st-century ivory trade. "They're made from plastic, not ivory," she blurted out before she could stop herself.

"Plas – s – tik" repeated the boy. "I have never heard of such a stone. This is remarkable! And how is it possible to dip each braid in molten silver without burning your hair?"

"This isn't silver," she explained, feeling slightly more confident as she rubbed the metal between her fingers. "This is kitchen foil. I cut it into squares, fold it around the tip of my hair, thread it through the bead, like a needle, and then bend it back into the bead to secure it."

"Kee- chen – foi – al," gasped Artafarnah. "This is wondrous! I have never seen a metal that can be worked with just fingers rather than a furnace. And your clothing," he continued, pointing at her leggings, "they suggest that your people are accomplished in horsemanship. Are you?

"I am," he boasted without even waiting for an answer. "I have been riding since the age of five. It is Persian tradition for all boys to be instructed in three things – to ride a horse, to draw a bow and to speak the truth. I am immensely proud and honoured that my name – Arta – means truth for we believe that the most disgraceful thing in the world is to tell a lie."

"I can ride a bike," answered Laurella truthfully but a little defensively. "It's a type of metal horse, popular throughout Albion. You sit on a saddle like a horse, but it has two wheels rather than four legs. I move my legs up and down to command it forward. I can't move it backwards, but I can make it rear up like a horse – we call it 'doing a wheelie'."

"A by-k!" the boy exclaimed, his eyes wide with wonder. "Did you hear that Zareen?" The cub glanced up at both children and responded with a gaping yawn. "Your country sounds like a strange but fascinating land," continued the boy. "I should like to visit it one day and do a wee - leeee."

"Indeed," smiled Laurella through gritted teeth, uncomfortable in the knowledge that this was highly unlikely – if not impossible – and desperate to change the subject before her flimsy cover was blown. "But please Artafarnah, will you tell me more about today's feast?"

"Certainly," beamed the boy, delighted to take on such an important task. "Every year nobles from across the Achaemenid Empire – from the Mediterranean in the West to the Indus River in the East – travel here to our capital Pasargadae to honour our King, Cyrus the Great, and feast with him.

"But my father has had to leave Pasargadae on urgent business for the King, so I have been given the privilege of attending the feast with my mother, here in this magnificent palace."

Brimming over with pride, Artafarnah suddenly clasped Laurella's hand in his and squeezed her fingers excitedly.

"Come Laurella, my dear new friend, walk with me and Zareen around the grounds and I shall show you so much more!"

Chapter 5

The trio began to weave a path through the crowd of adults, stopping intermittently to allow the cub to right herself when her soft paws slid on the highly polished floor. Laurella noticed that she still bore slight traces of camouflage spots on her back and legs. She was still only a baby.

They eventually reached the doorway, guarded on either side by towering stone bulls and stepped out into bright sunshine. They were now in a vast walled courtyard, filled with more adults – and more soldiers.

Laurella looked anxiously around her. "Are you certain it's alright for us to be here?" she whispered, making sure to avoid eye contact with any of the adults. She didn't think the guards looked like the kind of people who would take too kindly to a couple of children roaming around the place with a lion in tow.

"Please don't worry Laurella," Artafarnah reassured her, crouching down to tickle Zareen's round, silky tummy. The cub rolled in the warm earth and purred with delight. "These men are Immortals, and we are perfectly safe in their presence because my mother Pantea is their Commander and Chief, as is my father General Aryasb.

"The Immortals are the bravest of warriors on the battlefield. They are as formidable with the arrow as they are with the sword and in times of peace, they form the King's Royal Guard. It is a great honour to be an Immortal and I sincerely hope that one day I too shall have the privilege of leading them."

"Why are they called Immortals?" Laurella asked.

Artafarnah stood up and leaned closer to Laurella to reveal the answer. "Because they are kept constantly at a strength of exactly 10,000 men. Any warrior killed or seriously wounded is immediately replaced by another so, you see, the enemy can never defeat them for they will rise up again and again and again as if they are indeed immortal."

Laurella noticed how his words almost echoed Joy's theory of everlasting life – a perpetual regrouping of atoms that never die. She also found it ironic and somewhat sad that, despite the thousands of years that separated her life from Artafarnah's, nations were still hell-bent on fighting each other.

Shaking herself from her philosophical

ponderings Laurella's thoughts moved to Pantea. "I hope you don't mind me asking this Artafarnah but how did your mother become the leader of such a ... formidable force?"

"Because of her unquestionable valour and exceptional military expertise, of course!" he answered, somewhat baffled by her need to ask the question at all. "She is a fair and just commander who has earned the respect and loyalty of her men."

"Oh, I see," interrupted Laurella apologetically but Artafarnah continued.

"She is as brave as a lion and as shrewd as a fox, and her beauty is legendary," he proclaimed. "In fact, she must keep her face covered in battle to prevent the enemy from falling in love with her – OW, ZAREEN! Will you please stop doing that!" The cub had pounced on the boy and sunk her sharp teeth and claws into his bottom.

Laurella looked down at her trainers, desperately trying to stifle a giggle that threatened to erupt from her lips at any moment and reverberate around the magnificent courtyard. *Serves you right for showing off!* she thought. *Seriously, fancy saying your mum must cover her face to stop blood-thirsty warriors falling in love with her!* But despite all his boastings Laurella couldn't help but like him.

"Why do you ask this question?" inquired

Artafarnah, rubbing the back of his robe as a triumphant Zareen resumed her earlier position and waited for another tummy tickle. "Is your mother not a brave and fierce warrior?"

Laurella had to stifle another snigger. Her mum worked from home, writing blogs, web pages and other online information. She could be ferocious alright — especially when the internet went down, or her laptop froze — but Laurella couldn't exactly picture her mum racing into battle with 10,000 screaming Immortals at her side!

"No, my mother is a sort of scribe," she said, thinking of a way to describe a freelance writer to an ancient Persian. "But there are brave female warriors in my land too. I asked the question because some countries don't really see women as being equal to men."

"We do," Artafarnah answered assuredly. "Women are just as important as men in our society. They control and advance our glorious empire in partnership with men. They share the same professions, and they are paid equally for their labours."

"Now it's my turn to ask you a question," smiled Artafarnah. "Tell me about your father, Laurella. What position does he hold in your land?"

Her dad was an engineer by profession, but he

was one of those people who could turn his hand to anything and be really good at it; he was creative and practical.

"He's an engineer who oversees the running of many important buildings," she said proudly. "He's kind and he works with my mother, sharing chores and decisions...they're kinda calm actually."

"Calm?" repeated Artafarnah. "Do you mean like calm weather – tranquil and free from wind?"

"Not entirely," laughed Laurella. "And they're definitely not free from wind! 'Calm' is a word that people of my age use in my land when we want to say that someone is chilled and laid back."

"Then should they not sit upright in order to avoid the cold?" suggested Artafarnah, now completely confused.

"No," laughed Laurella, "I don't mean it literally. I suppose what I'm trying to say is that I admire them...and I love them."

"Then I should like to meet these calm, laid back individuals," smiled Artafarnah with genuine enthusiasm. "Where are they at the moment?"

Laurella's heart froze. How could she explain that she was here, one her own, with no mum and dad without raising the suspicions of a boy whose warrior parents were in charge of security?

"They're in another room at the moment," she

said quickly and honestly, reminded of Joy's words. "But I don't know which one."

"Don't worry, I'm sure you'll find them presently," said Artafarnah. "My father is a kind man too. He rescued Zareen and brought her back to me after her mother was killed."

"Killed?" repeated Laurella in alarm. "What happened to her?"

"She was hiding in long grass with Zareen," replied Artafarnah, looking down at the cub. "My father didn't see her because they were so well camouflaged. He must have got too close to them and she sprang out of her hiding place and tried to attack his horses, but she stumbled and got crushed by his chariot. She was only trying to protect her cub.

"Father heard Zareen calling to her mother and found her in the grass. She was only a few days old. She'd have died too if he had left her there."

"Oh, you poor thing," exclaimed Laurella, sinking to her knees and gathering the bewildered lion cub in her arms. She shuddered at the thought of ever losing her own mum or dad and hugged the cub tighter, forgetting all about pet etiquette or the risk of being bitten. Zareen seemed to sense Laurella's concern and gently licked her cheek with a tongue as rough as sandpaper.

"Thank goodness she has you to look after her now," she said, looking up at Artafarnah.

"I will always care for her," Artafarnah replied solemnly, crouching down to tickle the cub under her chin. "She's part of my family now."

He rose to his feet and the cub followed suit. "Enough of these sad thoughts – it's the King's birthday, after all," he smiled. "I'll help you find your parents. I promise. They can't be too far away, but first," he continued, clasping Laurella's hand once more, "let me take you to my favourite part of the palace: The King's Garden."

Chapter 6

The trio raced across the courtyard, their shadows stretching far before them as if eager to reach the garden first. Laurella looked up at the ancient blue sky, felt the glorious heat of the sun on her skin and then glanced at the Persian boy at her side. This had to be the most extraordinary holiday friendship ever!

As they walked under another carved gateway, guarded by two colossal gilt lions, the opulent scent of jasmine and roses filled Laurella's nostrils and made her feel blissfully happy. The sheer beauty of the place was breath-taking.

Lemon, lime and orange groves marked the four corners of the walled garden, their vibrant fruit shimmering like jewels against the dark waxy foliage. Elsewhere pink pomegranates hung like Christmas baubles from drooping branches, purple figs nodded gently in the warm breeze and walnuts peeped out from their fleshy protective cases. Grapevines, laden with frosted green and purple fruit, clung to the walls while tiny, white stars of jasmine and red velvet rosebuds snaked their way up the masonry to bask in the sunshine. Tall Cyprus trees guarded the verdant space like elegant sentries and in perfectly symmetrical beds flowed rivers of lavender, rosemary, laurel, oregano, sage, and thyme.

In the centre was a raised rectangular pond, speckled with circular lily pad rafts and flamboyant pink blooms. Iridescent dragonflies danced over its flat, mirrored surface and gloried in the reflected beauty of the garden.

"Wow! This place is ab-so-lutely stunning," said Laurella, as she slowly pivoted, both arms outstretched, to enable all of her senses to drink up the astonishing beauty.

"The King calls it his paradise," beamed Artafarnah, delighted that his friend loved the garden as much as he did. "He tends it himself."

Laurella sat, cross-legged, on the pristine gravel and was soon joined by Zareen who stretched out, sphinx-like, before her.

"Why did you call her Zareen," asked Laurella, stroking the lion cub's head and shoulders. Zareen purred loudly.

"It means 'made of gold' answered Artafarnah. Laurella thought it a perfect name for such a special pet.

The cub closed her eyes and dozed in the sunshine but awoke instantly when Laurella rustled the end of her leash, trapping it effortlessly with one swipe of her paw.

"She's just like a kitten playing with string," said Laurella as the cub's wide eyes watched every twist and turn of the leash.

"She loves that game," smiled Artafarnah. "We play it here often. The garden is the only place in the palace where she's allowed to roam free.

"Few people have seen this very private part of the palace but the King, in his graciousness, allows me to visit it whenever I like," he continued proudly, walking over to the pond, and sitting on the raised stone perimeter. Mother loves the garden too and this is our favourite spot."

As Artafarnah dipped his hand into the still, cool water circular ripples radiated out across the surface – just like the invisible waves that had drawn Laurella back through time.

"For some reason, I always feel attracted to water," he said, glancing up at Laurella with a look that said that he had not shared this thought with anyone else. "It makes me feel tranquil and content but sometimes a little sad too."

"I know exactly what you mean," said Laurella excitedly, delighted at this shared experience. "I get the same feeling, especially when I'm near the sea, but I can't explain why." The reason was simple. Although South Londoners through and through, her parents both shared an island heritage. Her mum had been born in Jersey and her dad's parents had come from Jamaica. The sea was in her blood.

The children fell silent for a moment, reflecting on the phenomenon. But they were soon brought back to their senses by the sound of Zareen lapping water from the pond, her pink tongue turning the ripples into tiny waves.

"Clever girl Zareen, you've given me an idea," said Artafarnah. "Laurella, let's build ships from leaves and twigs then see how far they can sail across the pond. Orange leaves make the finest hulls and I know just where to find the best ones!" With that, he jumped up from his seat and disappeared into the foliage with Zareen close by his side.

Enjoying the warmth of the sunshine, Laurella stretched her arms out lazily and ambled over to a nearby rosemary bush. Leaning over, she gently rubbed its leaves between her fingers to release its aromatic oil.

"HOW DARE YOU TRESPASS IN THE KING'S GARDEN!" roared a voice behind her. The sudden noise shocked several glossy starlings from the branches of an olive tree and almost sent Laurella

36

flying headfirst into the rosemary.

She spun around to see a thick-set man in rich red Persian robes, his face contorted with rage. He had the cruellest eyes that Laurella had ever seen and their intense malevolence made her blood run cold.

"You are right to be afraid, wretch," he snarled, jabbing a stubby index finger into her chest to accentuate every word, "for now you will face the most dire of consequences."

Wide-eyed and speechless Laurella stumbled backwards as the man loomed over her. There was no escape. She was trapped.

Chapter 7

Hearing the sudden commotion, Artafarnah raced back and pushed himself between Laurella and the Persian. Zareen crouched by Laurella's side, flattened her ears to her head and let out a low, long rumbling growl.

"She is my guest General Vidarna," Artafarnah shouted indignantly, "and as such she is perfectly entitled to be here with me."

"How is it," continued the general, addressing Artafarnah now but not taking his dreadful eyes off Laurella, "that you two dare to scuttle around these private grounds with that filthy animal on such an important day as this? I should be focusing on important affairs of state but instead, my attention has been diverted here to flush you out like the vermin you are."

Laurella clenched both fists and dug her nails into both palms as briny tears of anger and frustration suddenly welled up in her eyes and threatened to overflow. She could do nothing to defend herself for if she uttered a single word her cover would be blown. *Who is this man? And what exactly is his problem?* she thought through gritted teeth. She tried to glare back at him, using what her dad would describe as her best 'Paddington stare' but his brutal eyes forced her to look away.

"We're entitled to be here, and we are doing no wrong so I would be obliged if you would refrain from insulting my guest," persisted Artafarnah bravely. "Pantea, my mother said that I..."

"Your mother?" interrupted the general, spitting the words out as if they were poison. "Of course, the brave Commander of the Immortals who can't even control her feral son.

"GET OUT OF MY SIGHT THIS MOMENT!" he screamed, lunging towards Artafarnah. "AND TAKE THIS GIRL WITH YOU BEFORE I BEAT THE IMPUDENCE OUT OF YOU! IF I CATCH YOU IN THE GARDEN AGAIN WITH THAT CREATURE OFF ITS LEASH, I'LL HAVE IT DROWNED!"

Artafarnah scooped the cub up under one arm, quickly grabbed Laurella's hand and together they sprinted from the garden. Although he tried desperately to hide it Laurella saw the humiliation, shame and fury in Artafarnah's eyes – and her heart raged in sympathy.

Chapter 8

Once they were a safe distance away from the general the friends skidded to a halt and tried to catch their breath. Panting heavily with her hands on her hips, Laurella looked back at the garden and then at Artafarnah. He placed Zareen gently on the ground and remained focused on the cub, deliberately avoiding Laurella's gaze. She began to fumble with the laces of her left trainer and eventually plucked out a chunk of gravel, which had been flicked up under the tongue in her haste to escape from the garden. It was almost clear, like crystal, and had straight edges on one side. Laurella decided to keep it.

"Thank you for defending me back there," she said, finally breaking the uncomfortable silence. "You are a good and honourable person, unlike that horrible man. Your parents must be very proud to have you as their son."

She hoped her carefully chosen words would help to ease his embarrassment. She also wanted him to take strength from the knowledge that they now had a shared contempt for a mutual enemy.

"Who is General Vidarna anyway and why does he appear to hate us so much?" Laurella asked.

"I'm so sorry that you had to endure that injustice, Laurella," said Artafarnah, as Zareen nuzzled his hand with her cheek. "General Vidarna has treated me with contempt for as long as I can remember but I have no idea why. His behaviour is always at its worst when he finds me alone with Zareen and he always manages to twist situations to make it appear that I am in the wrong. He says nothing when I'm with my parents though; he simply looks through me as if I don't exist."

"He sounds like a coward and a bully to me." declared Laurella. "Have you told your parents about his behaviour?"

The boy nodded but looked slightly embarrassed as if he felt telling his parents was a sign of weakness. "Mother dislikes him intensely and father doesn't trust him but, thankfully, we see him very rarely because he is based far from here in Susa. He reports to the governor there and keeps the citizens in order," he said.

"I pity those poor people," said Laurella. "It sounds to me like General Vidarna is jealous of the King's respect for your parents and so he takes his frustrations out on you as only a coward would."

"Yes," agreed Artafarnah, "He could never lead the Immortals – for he lacks a lion's heart!"

The young cub flicked her tail contemptuously and attempted a roar but could only muster a high-pitched squeak. The sound melted Laurella's heart.

A huge smile lit up Artafarnah face once more. "Exactly my little warrior," he laughed, playfully rubbing the cub's head. "You're far braver than he could ever be!

"The great feast will be starting soon," he added, turning to Laurella. "Let us go now to the Banqueting Hall. I'm sure we'll find your parents there." Laurella knew differently.

"The feast will last for many hours, so mother has promised to take me and Zareen out to the garden for a while," continued Artafarnah. "Do you think your parents will permit you to join us?"

"I'm certain they will," smiled Laurella.

As the trio neared the Banqueting Hall they came to a spectacular double staircase, richly decorated with painted stone reliefs of peoples from all parts of the empire bearing gifts for the king. The beautifully carved figures wore the same varied regional dress as the adults that Laurella had first spied in the Hall of all Nations. She also noticed a dramatic double frieze at the base of each staircase which depicted a powerful lion sinking its ferocious teeth and claws into a terrified bull. The striking image reminded her of Zareen's mother. The thought made her shudder.

Pointing proudly to the carved figures, Artafarnah said: "We govern all of our territories on the principle of equal rights for all and respect for all cultures. All we ask in return is that every subject of our glorious Empire pays their taxes and lives peacefully."

Laurella couldn't help but feel that his proclamation was a recital of the 'official' adult viewpoint. And although his words were full of genuine conviction, Laurella wasn't sure that 'glorious' was the right way to describe any kind of empire that ruled over other people – whether they liked it or not. But it wasn't the right time, or the right place in time to start that kind of conversation and, besides, the last thing she wanted to do was to offend a friend who had offered her nothing but kindness.

As they began to climb the stairs Laurella noticed a small area with strange triangular markings, like tiny arrows or thorns pressed into the stone. "What's this?" she asked.

Artafarnah looked slightly confused at the question. "It's cuneiform of course. Are you not able to read?" he inquired, with no hint of ridicule.

"Yes, I can read very well," answered Laurella, realising for the first time that she must – of course – be speaking in Ancient Persian, but she had no idea how she could speak and understand it so fluently. "But in Albion, we use a different set of symbols. We call it the alphabet. What does the cuneiform say?"

"It bids all visitors welcome to the Banqueting Hall," Artafarnah beamed. "That gives me an idea. Would you like me to show you what your name looks like in my writing? We usually press our words into soft clay, but I will try another method."

"Yes please," she replied. "And I can show you what your name looks like in my writing – and Zareen's too!"

The trio ran back down the steps and selected a soft patch of earth by the side of the staircase. And as Zareen looked on in fascination, the friends began to press in and scratch out their names, using the piece of gravel that Laurella had kept in her hand.

When they were finished Laurella and Artafarnah stood back to examine their work. "Just a minute; we mustn't forget Zareen's special signature," said Laurella, crouching down to draw a paw print under the names. And, with one final flourish, she enclosed the words within a large, neat heart. She didn't know why – it just felt right.

"Perfect," smiled Artafarnah. "Now let's eat!"

The trio reached the top of the staircase and approached an immense doorway, guarded by two magnificent, winged creatures – half-man, half-bull – each hair of their beards exquisitely carved and each delicate feather picked out with gold leaf. Laurella stood at the hall's marble threshold and her jaw fell open at the sheer scale of its dimensions. The room was filled with a forest of enormous columns stretching up to a sky of lapis blue and gold. From the top of each column carved bulls and lions looked down from their scrolled platforms while giant eagles spread their golden wings across the painted walls.

An infinite fleet of wooden tables and benches fanned out from one vast top table, its sturdy wooden legs beautifully crafted into the shape of upright, roaring lions. Behind it stood two ornate wooden thrones with intricate carvings, red velvet seats and backrests and matching footstools.

Laurella gazed about her fantastical surroundings and watched the hall begin to fill with representatives from every part of the ancient empire. As they milled towards the tables Laurella's eyes were drawn to a beautiful woman with dark flowing curls. Her Persian gown was a shimmering aquamarine and around her neck hung a gold pendant shaped like the head of a lioness. She approached the children, smiling warmly.

"So, there you are my dearest," she laughed, gently stroking the side of Artafarnah's face.

"Laurella," beamed Artafarnah, "may I introduce you to my mother Pantea, brave warrior of the Achaemenid and Commander of the Immortals. And mother, may I introduce you to my dear new friend Laurella, a citizen of the Cat Ford in the Kingdom of..."

"I'm very pleased to meet you," interrupted Laurella, grabbing Pantea's hand and shaking it a little too vigorously. She knew that Pantea would know instantly that the kingdom of Albion was not part of their empire, and then she would start asking questions, and then Laurella's cover would be blown sky-high.

Amused by the girl's over-enthusiastic but well-meaning greeting, Pantea wrapped her free hand around Laurella's fingers, gently enclosed the girl's hand in hers and finally brought the manic handshaking to an end.

"I am very pleased to meet you too Laurella," she smiled, looking deeply into Laurella's eyes. "A friend who is dear to Artafarnah is dear to me also, so I bid you a warm welcome to Pasargadae. I confess I know little of your city of Cat Ford, but I hope to be able to discover more with help from you and your parents later this evening perhaps? But now, I am afraid that you will have to excuse us for we have to prepare for the feast. Would you like us to take you to your parents before we depart?"

"No thank you," trilled Laurella, desperately trying to sound calm and relaxed. "I'm sure I'll be able to find them."

Pantea smiled in acknowledgement and began to lead her son away. Zareen trotted confidently behind them —and then promptly did the splits on the polished stone floor. Artafarnah giggled and turned back to face Laurella. "Don't forget to ask your parents about the garden," he cried.

"Don't worry, I won't!" Laurella called back. *And I won't forget that close shave in a hurry either,* she thought to herself as she breathed out a massive sigh of relief.

Chapter 9

"Behold Cyrus the Great, King of the World, great King; legitimate King, King of Babylon, King of Sumer and Akkad, King of the four rims of the Earth!" the Royal Herald bellowed. With these words, the Great Banqueting hall fell silent.

Laurella, positioned once more behind one of the huge outer pink pillars, peeped out from her hiding place to see Cyrus the Great and his Queen Cassandane walk regally towards their thrones. The King was a tall, handsome man with olive skin, dark curly hair and a luxuriously long, curly beard. He wore a magnificent crimson belted robe, edged with an embroidered gold border, and from his belt hung an ornate dagger enclosed in a jewel-encrusted sheath. His tall golden crown was a breath-taking marvel of exquisite metalwork, with flowing shapes and patterns that almost appeared to have a life of their own. His Queen wore a lilac robe so fine and delicate that it could have been spun from the gossamer thread of a spider's web, bejewelled with morning dew. She had kind, dark eyes and long, tight curls. Her diadem was a smaller but equally beautiful version of her husband's crown and the pair wore gold hoop earrings and exquisitely carved gold griffon-headed bangles.

Cyrus and Cassandane sat down gracefully on their velvet cushions. Then the silence was broken as the hall rumbled to the tide of assorted regional robes cascading onto more than a thousand benches. And then the King spoke. His voice took Laurella totally by surprise. It was mesmerizingly deep and rich. Inexplicably, it reminded her of melted chocolate and the aromatic spicy aroma of shoe polish!

"Welcome one and all," he purred deeply, his lionesque tones reverberating effortlessly around the hall. "To those that have travelled far and wide, we are grateful for your presence and to those that have laboured long and hard to prepare such a feast we are grateful for your toil. So, let us now all sit together and eat!"

Laurella was taken by surprise once more. She wasn't expecting such good manners from an ancient king. *I bet Henry VIII didn't say 'thank you' very often,* she thought to herself as the most wonderful smells started to waft enticingly into her nostrils, instantly triggering loud, grumbling protestations from the pit of her stomach.

She was absolutely starving but she couldn't simply sit down at a table and tuck in, however much she wanted to. An elaborate feast like this would have an equally elaborate seating plan and she definitely wasn't down on the list. *You'll just have to wait until it's safe to eat,* she told herself firmly. *Artafarnah's bound to be able to smuggle something delicious out later,* she hoped.

Laurella had a brainwave. She might have a sweet in her jacket pocket. She'd often find a long-forgotten ultra-sour fizzy jelly, boiled sweet or even a cola flavoured lolly languishing in the lining. But would she be lucky today? Her mouth watered as she plundered her pockets expectantly... but her jacket was a sugar-free wasteland containing just her inedible smartphone and earphones.

That's it! she rallied. *If I can't eat the feast, I'll film it. And then I can show Joy and Mum and Dad and prove that I was really here... in Ancient Persia... at the flippin birthday feast of Cyrus the Great!*

Taking great care not to be seen, Laurella carefully positioned her phone, zoomed right in, and started to pan around the great hall. A never-ending army of men and women clad all in white brought out endless dishes of mouth-watering exotic fare, each more enticing than the last.

Who are you lot then? Im-morsels? she smirked inwardly, delighted at her joke.

She decided to focus on the feast. She saw huge silver platters piled high with succulent, roasted meats and wicker baskets overflowing with crusty, warm bread that gave a satisfying crunch when torn apart. She saw ornate silver tureens filled with the most delicious smelling casserole, infused with fresh herbs, saffron, pistachio nuts and sultanas, with meat so tender it looked like it would simply melt on the tongue. As if that wasn't enough to torment her taste buds, endless side dishes of almonds, juicy pomegranates, ripe figs, golden honey, apples, pears, plump raisins and dates danced before her hungry eyes.

Diners carefully held a piece of bread in their left hands and then used a knife in their right hands to select their chosen toppings before placing the gorgeous combinations into their mouths. As the thousands of diners ate gratefully their silver drinking bowls were re-filled with wine, poured from silver horn-shaped jugs decorated at their bases with exquisite, winged griffons.

Laurella put her video on pause, repositioned herself at the other side of the pillar and resumed filming, hoping to capture more delicious Persian fayre. Instead, she spied General Vidarna who stabbed at his food disdainfully and glared menacingly at any diner sharing his table who attempted to make polite conversation with him.

Oh, it's you, you rude pig, thought Laurella bitterly, still smarting from her earlier encounter with the general. *Seems like you have the table manners of a pig too!* she deliberated, zooming in the video closer to prove her suspicions.

He really was an obnoxious man. He tore at his food and ate open-mouthed as if chewing a rancid hunk of gristle. When his table was offered more wine, he thrust up his drinking bowl to ensure he was served first and then barked insults at the wine pourer as he demanded constant re-fills.

Suddenly the general jumped up from his bench, sending his plate and drinking bowl careering off the table. Making no attempt to retrieve them, he stormed away from the startled diners.

Good riddance to bad rubbish! called Laurella inwardly as he strode towards the gargantuan doorway. His sudden exit reminded her of her promise to Artafarnah, so she stopped filming and put her phone safely away in her jacket pocket.

It must be about time to meet up now, she assured herself. *It won't matter if I'm a bit early.* She really needed to get away from all the gorgeous food.

With precise, svelte steps Laurella made her

way towards the doorway, ensuring she remained concealed in the shadows as she jumped from outer pillar to outer pillar. She eventually reached the magnificently carved archway and headed out into the twilight; her tiny figure completely dwarfed by the colossal stone sentries.

Well, that was pretty easy, she said to herself as she skipped down the vast staircase. She stepped onto the courtyard and breathed in the warm, perfumed air. As she stood in the stillness, she closed her eyes to appreciate the exotic hum of cicadas singing their evening chorus.

"HALT! WHO GOES THERE?" screamed a voice, just millimetres from her ear. Laurella felt as if she'd been struck by lightning. Every tendon in her body tensed up, temporarily transforming the 10-year-old into a wide-eyed gargoyle, teeth bared and fingers flexed.

Seriously! What IS IT with you Ancient Persians and unexpected announcements? she asked herself angrily. This was the third time she'd been scared out of her skin that day.

Can't you just say 'excuse me' like any normal person? she grumbled inwardly.

Laurella regained her composure and turned to face the origin of the offensive sound. He was a beautifully dressed, heavily armed Immortal and, by the steely look in his brown eyes, he wanted an answer from her – fast.

"I am Laurella from the Kingdom of Albion," she announced, hoping that he hadn't detected the slight tremble in her voice. "I am on my way to the King's Garden for I have been invited there by Pantea, brave warrior of the Achaemenid and Commander of the Immortals."

On hearing the girl utter his Commander's name the Immortal stiffened immediately as if standing to attention. "You may go," he told her and then stared straight ahead as if he'd been turned to stone.

"Thank you," she replied as she started to stride purposefully across the deserted courtyard.

That, Laurella Swift, was way too close for comfort, she warned herself, as her heart pounded ferociously in her chest. She could even hear the blood pumping through her ears. She was afraid the whole world could hear her heartbeat. It felt so loud she feared it might even drown out the cicadas.

The Immortal watched Laurella make her way towards the garden and then glanced down at a patch of disturbed ground near the base of the staircase. It puzzled him. It looked like the remnants of words and other markings pressed and scratched into the earth, now almost obliterated as if someone had deliberately tried to stamp them out.

* * *

In the still of the garden, Pantea stood by a pomegranate tree, laden with ripe fruit. She watched as Artafarnah sat happily by the pond with his loyal cub at his feet, gently scooping up handfuls of water then letting the liquid casually escape through his fingers.

She loved these rare moments of simplicity, for here they could just be mother and son, together in solitude, sharing the breath-taking beauty of the garden. She smiled at his innocence and then turned to select the biggest, ripest fruit for her beautiful boy.

Artafarnah gazed up from the water and smiled as he saw his mother's silhouette against the dappled green foliage. Zareen snored gently in her sleep. He loved this place at twilight. It was so peaceful and safe and magical.

He turned back to the pond's mirrored surface, hoping to spot the first bright star in the night sky. But, instead, he saw the flash of a blade and felt its razor-sharp edge at his throat. Then the terrified boy saw the looming reflection and cruel eyes of General Vidarna.

Chapter 10

With her heartbeat now stabilised and a renewed taste for adventure, Laurella skipped happily into the garden, eager to share more of its beauty with her fascinating new friend. But instead, she was confronted with the ugly brutality of a deadly stand-off.

Pantea stood, dagger drawn, with every muscle tensed. She waited, ready to pounce. Little Zareen cowered by her feet, her top lip curled into a silent snarl. Even in the failing light, Laurella could see Pantea's dark eyes burning with molten hatred for the man who held her son. Facing her, General Vidarna gloried in her frustration and helplessness. He stared back at her defiantly and licked his lips as if savouring the fear that coursed through the captive boy's veins.

Shocked by the grotesque tableau, Laurella darted into the waxy green camouflage of an orange bush and prayed no-one had heard her. A tsunami of terror rushed through her body. Clasping her hand over her mouth, she frantically tried to stifle her panicked breaths and wished, more than anything, in her whole life, to be back in the little Freshwater chalet with her mum and dad.

Zareen tried to edge forward, shoulders hunched and belly close to the ground, but her advance was halted when the general kicked a shower of gravel in her face.

"And so here we have this exquisite conundrum," leered General Vidarna, tightening his grip on Artafarnah.

"Here stands Pantea, fearless Commander of the Immortals, now rendered powerless like her pathetic little lion cub – and all because of her pitiful love for her whelp.

Zareen hissed, wide-eyed and ears flat but Pantea remained silent, her eyes still fixed on the general.

"Your duty and loyalty should be to your King, and your King alone," the general proclaimed pompously. "You should be at his side day and night, protecting him from all evil, putting his welfare above all others but instead, you dare to come here, choosing your son over the King!

"But yet, why should this surprise me?" he added with an air of false pity. "You are but a mere woman, totally out of her depth in a man's world. Only a woman would leave the King's banquet to

57

play frivolous games with her worthless offspring."

"Don't you dare talk to me about loyalty," snarled Pantea. "You care nothing for your King and Empire; your only concern is your own advancement. It is no secret that you will stop at nothing to further your career – and don't think your barbarous style of 'law enforcement' in Susa is not known to the King, for he is greatly displeased.

"The King chose me to lead the Immortals – not you – and you simply can't bear to face that fact. Your pathetic quarrel is with me and me alone and I will happily face you in battle. What have you got to fear, I am but a 'mere woman' after all? Gather up the last vestiges of honour that you possess and let my son go and then we can settle this here and now. That's what you want, isn't it?"

Laurella listened to their conversation with growing terror. She desperately wanted to run away but, at the same time, she couldn't leave her friend. She felt frozen in a deadly nightmare, unable to help and unable to escape.

"Oh, if only it were that simple," the general laughed cruelly, pressing the knife even closer into Artafarnah's throat. "You have failed in your duty to protect the King and I will prove it here and now. An assassin has been sent to kill the King, tonight, at his birthday banquet. I have this information from exemplary sources. You should be in the hall protecting him now; putting your life before his but instead you have the audacity to relax here in the king's own garden!

"AND LOOK! YOU REMAIN HERE STILL, EVEN THOUGH I HAVE JUST TOLD YOU THAT YOUR KING IS IN MORTAL DANGER!" the general roared. "Your shameful inaction amounts to treason and the penalty for treason is death. Your treachery stems from your pitiful love for your son and so it is your son who must die!"

Chapter 11

Overcome by blind panic, Laurella rushed out from her leafy hiding place and screamed a roar that was petrifying and primaeval.

"YOU ARE A LIAR!" she cried, her eyes wild and wide. "You know the King is safe, protected by the Immortals, but you – General Vidarna – you are not safe at all, for you are now in immortal danger!"

Scrambling for her smartphone, she hit play on the video and held the phone aloft.

"I am Laurella, keeper of souls and I now possess yours!" she screamed. The startled Persians froze in horror as they watched the general's moving form, lit up in the twilight by the phone's ethereal glow. She had indeed captured his soul.

Inwardly, terror coursed through every vein of Laurella's body – and by the look on all three Persians' faces, she struck the same terror in theirs. She had no idea if Vidarna was telling the truth about the assassin or not, but she had to call his bluff to save her friend.

"Release the boy immediately or I will destroy

your soul in an instant and you will roam this earth for all eternity, unable to rest and unable to find peace. You will be nothing but a decaying hollow husk, no longer living but unable to die!"

Laurella didn't know what she was saying but the words just kept tumbling out of her mouth. She hovered her thumb menacingly over the delete button and as she thrust the phone towards the general, he immediately dropped his blade, crumpled to his knees and then curled, hands over his head, into a cowering ball.

"Mercy!" the general whimpered, his voice muffled by the gravelled path pressed against his sweating, clammy face. "I confess that I lied about the King. There is no assassin. He is in no danger."

Artafarnah scrambled to safety and Pantea rushed forward, dagger aloft. Zareen sprang into the boy's arms and he held her close, squeezing his eyes tight shut.

"Stop Pantea!" Laurella cried. "The general belongs to me!"

Pantea skidded to a halt, showering a hail of gravel over the general's huddled form. As she stared at Laurella, panting to catch her breath, Artafarnah rushed to his mother's side and was immediately wrapped in her arms.

Laurella had to think quickly. She despised

General Vidarna, but she knew Pantea would kill him and she couldn't have that on her conscience. She was also terrified at the petrifying thought of witnessing a bloody and violent death.

Desperate to maintain her mask of divine aloofness, Laurella forced herself to look down disdainfully at the general. "Your lying and treachery are out of control and now you have added drunken violence to your list of crimes," she declared, trying to think of how a god would speak.

"I should destroy you now... but, I may still show you mercy. You have until dawn to get as far away from this palace as possible. So, saddle up your horse and keep on riding. Take yourself beyond the furthest boundaries of this empire and never dare to return. Live your life in peace from this moment onwards and harm no other. I will be watching you constantly and if you ever threaten another soul, I will devour yours!"

On hearing her blood-curdling oath the general scrambled to his feet and scurried from the garden, stumbling over his feet in his haste to reach the palace stables.

Zareen wriggled free from Artafarnah's arms and chased after the general. A few moments later, Laurella heard a yowling shriek of pain and, in the distance, through the gateway, she saw that the lion cub had latched herself on to the general's right calf. It wasn't one of her playful nips. This time it looked like she wanted to teach him a lesson he'd never forget.

Chapter 12

As nightfall slowly filled the garden, a sense of renewed calm began to envelop Laurella and soothe her jangled nerves. But Pantea and Artafarnah still stared, transfixed, at the strange solitary girl. Zareen trotted back into the garden and tried to make her way towards Laurella but was immediately scooped up into Artafarnah's arms.

Laurella took a deep breath and broke the uneasy silence. "I know that truth is the most important thing for you so I must confess that everything I just said to General Vidarna was a lie," she said.

Pantea's eyes widened and Artafarnah's mouth gaped open as Laurella continued, "I'm not the keeper of souls. I'm just a normal girl, on my own... out of my depth.

"And this," she added, holding up her phone, "is not a magic talisman. It's just something made by ordinary men and women. It's called a phone where I come from. It records information, in the same way as your clay tablets do, I suppose, but this type of tablet is made from metal and plastic."

"Pla-s-tic? Like the pla-s-tic beads in your hair?" suggested Artafarnah cautiously, still totally bewildered by what had just happened.

"Yes, exactly," smiled Laurella, delighted that she hadn't struck her friend permanently dumb with terror. "Just as the water in the pond captures your reflection, my phone can capture your likeness, but it is just your moving image, not your soul. I said all that stuff about souls because I thought the general was going to kill you. I was terrified for you – and for me – but I couldn't just hide back there in the bushes and do nothing."

She hesitated once more before continuing "I do come from Catford... but I don't come from your time."

On hearing this revelation, it was Pantea's turn to stare, open-mouthed, mirroring her son's incredulous expression.

Reminded of Joy's words, Laurella tried to explain how she was able to travel through time and dimensions and how she had used a key to pass from her dimension to theirs as if moving between rooms.

"I think my key drew me to your 'room' to save Artafarnah's life, but all of this is new to me too," she admitted. "I'm just an ordinary girl but, for some extraordinary reason, I can open these doors between our different dimensions... so, there it is...

that's the truth – I promise."

Pantea stood in silence, running her long fingers through Artafarnah's dark hair as if searching through his rich curls could help her find a way to make sense of what she had just heard.

"Your story is fantastical and almost beyond comprehension," she said at last. "But I know you speak the truth – it shines through your eyes. You are anything but an ordinary girl, Laurella of the Cat Ford – you have the courage of a lion and the quick wit of a fox. It took immense bravery and guile to free my son from the clutches of that deceitful dog and I will be forever indebted to you.

"I would be lying if I told you I didn't want the general dead. I still long to spill his cowardly blood but you found it in your heart to show him mercy and so I must and will honour your wishes."

"Your son is very courageous too," interjected Laurella, looking over at the now beaming Artafarnah. "He stood up to the general when he threatened me in this garden earlier today. He'd only just met me so he could have just left me, but he chose to stay by my side. That's what I call true friendship."

"Then come, my brave lion cubs," laughed Pantea, still cuddling Artafarnah and Zareen while stretching out her other arm to Laurella. "Let us embrace as one family and celebrate our newfound friendship that transcends time itself!" Laurella didn't need to be asked twice. She rushed to Pantea's side and hugged her tightly.

As the garden's sweet nocturnal perfume filled the air the fearless Achaemenid warrior breathed a sigh of maternal relief and two children from different worlds shared the universal security of feeling safe, at last, in a mother's arms.

Chapter 13

The trio ambled hand-in-hand out of the garden and Zareen padded alongside, rearing up occasionally in failed attempts to swat fireflies. Laurella looked up at the crescent moon and turned to Pantea. "It's getting late now so I probably should start to think about going home," she said. "But before I do could I ask you for one thing please?"

"Why, of course," replied Pantea, "What do you desire?"

"Could I have something to eat?" asked Laurella, smiling. "I've had nothing all day and I'm starving."

"Spoken like a true Achaemenid," laughed Pantea. And as the three friends made their way towards the Great Banqueting Hall their happy voices entwined and rose into the clear, star-studded night sky.

* * *

Laurella tore off a piece of warm crusty bread and dipped it into the bowl of rich, velvety stew. As the mahogany-coloured gravy touched her tongue, her taste buds fizzed with effervescent delight at the presence of cinnamon, then oregano, then garlic and even a hint of saffron and apricot. She had never tasted anything so delicious. Just as she'd imagined when spying the diners earlier that evening, each morsel of tender lamb really did melt in her mouth.

Something tugged at her leggings and Laurella looked down to see Zareen's large, amber eyes looking up at her expectantly. "Ah bless, are you hungry too?" she asked, dipping more bread into the stew, and passing it down to the cub. Zareen devoured it in an instant and tugged at Laurella's leggings once more.

"Leave her be Zareen," laughed Artafarnah. "Our dear friend has not eaten all day – unlike you!"

"Try these, Laurella" he encouraged, pushing over a small plate of roasted salted radishes. Laurella had only eaten them raw before but as she bit into the slightly caramelised pink and white balls, she was surprised to find that their spicy bite had mellowed, and they now tasted like juicy little potatoes.

"These are awesome," she smiled, holding her ornate silver drinking bowl to her lips and taking a small sip of sweet, diluted date wine.

Suddenly a golden paw appeared at the edge of the table, felt around frantically and then, with an expert flick, knocked the half-eaten bowl of stew onto the bench below.

"Oh Zareen, will you behave!" exclaimed Artafarnah, as the cheeky cub glanced up momentarily from the bowl, licked her lips and then resumed her feast.

"Try this then," smiled Artafarnah, offering another dish filled with small golden cubes in a thick, sticky sauce. "But beware of thieving paws!"

Laurella loved their sweet and spicy taste. "Mmm, this is gorgeous," she marvelled, helping herself to another heaped spoonful. "What is it?"

"Turnip," declared Artafarnah.

"Turnip?" spluttered Laurella. "I've never tasted turnip like this before." Her only previous experience of the humble vegetable had been in a disgusting mushy medley of frozen 'mixed veg'.

Pantea had chosen a quiet area to eat, far away from the King's top table. She knew sharing Laurella's unbelievable story with the rest of the diners would cause a stampede of inquisitiveness – and possibly alarm. Laurella had already had her fill of drama for one day – now she simply needed to fill her rumbling stomach.

"You must also try these sweetmeats, smiled Pantea, "These are Artafarnah's favourite and I have a feeling you will like them too."

Laurella's eyes were drawn to a platter of small

cakes and pastries, each soaked in golden honey and decorated with plump almonds, pistachios and fleshy pomegranate seeds. Pantea was right – they tasted divine, like bitesize pieces of warm summer sunshine.

"When you have had your fill, you must tell us more about your key," continued Pantea.

"I'll show you now if you like," answered Laurella, popping one last pastry into her mouth. "It's in the Hall of All Nations."

Chapter 14

The foursome walked back through the enormous, exquisitely carved doorway, guarded on either side by the two towering white bulls and re-entered the breath-taking Hall of All Nations.

"Now, where is it again?" pondered Laurella. "I remember. We need to find the seventh outer-most pillar topped by a golden lion by the west wall. I think it's over here."

She led her friends to the large, red banner adorned with the golden eagle. The golden threads started to glow and fizz as she approached and Laurella was immediately overcome with the same feeling of nausea that she had felt in the charity shop.

"I think it's time for me to go back," she said, turning sadly to her friends. She had a gut-wrenching feeling that their lives would never cross again, and they sensed it too. Her eyes started to glisten with tears as she realised the finality of the situation.

Stepping forward, Pantea unclipped her finely

carved golden lioness pendant and placed it around Laurella's neck.

She smiled, gently brushed one of the beaded braids away from Laurella's face and wiped away a solitary tear that had begun to trace a briny course down her cheek.

Then she said solemnly: "Laurella of the Cat Ford, brave warrior of Albion, know that you will always be a daughter of the Achaemenid. Go now in peace and safety with our love and eternal gratitude."

Artafarnah rushed forward and hugged Laurella tightly. Zareen bounded after him and rubbed her cheek against Laurella's leg, purring loudly. "Farewell my dear friend, I promise you will stay in my heart forever," he smiled, choking back tears.

"And I promise you will always stay in mine," replied Laurella. "And you too Zareen," she added, crouching down to give the cub one last cuddle. "I will never forget you Artafarnah and remember – we will only ever be rooms apart."

As she said the words, she noticed that her voice already sounded far away and echoing. She smiled one last time at Pantea, Artafarnah and Zareen as their figures, so tiny against the backdrop of the cavernous hall, slowly turned at right angles and

then suddenly splintered into a kaleidoscopic frieze
of multi-coloured hexagons.

Chapter 15

"Feeling better now darlin'?" enquired Joy anxiously.

At the sound of Joy's voice, Laurella opened her eyes and found herself back in the 21st-century surroundings of the charity shop in Freshwater. She tentatively put one hand to her neck and was ecstatic when her fingers touched the ancient lioness pendant.

"Oh Joy, you'll never believe what's just happened. I've just been to ancient Persia!" Laurella cried. "I've even filmed some of it, look!" she said, scrambling in her pocket to retrieve the phone. She hit the play button on the video app excitedly, but the video was blank. She tried again and again, frantically hitting the play button but there was no trace of her adventure.

"I don't understand it. I definitely filmed it all – the feast, the people...General Vidarna – but now it's just disappeared," wailed Laurella.

"Remember, time works differently in different dimensions darlin'," explained Joy. "You may have spent hours, even days in ancient Persia but in this dimension, you've only been away for a matter of seconds, at most."

Laurella looked up at the charity shop's gently ticking wall clock and saw, to her amazement, that it was still only seven minutes past eleven.

"That's why you can't play your video in this dimension," Joy continued. "But who needs a video when you've got a crystal-clear memory like yours and that stunning necklace. Now come sit on this stool here by the counter and tell me all about your travels."

Laurella began to recount her fantastic adventure to her captivated friend and confidante, making sure to include every last detail.

The tinkling brass shop bell heralded the arrival of Laurella's mum and dad.

"Hi, you two. How's things?" smiled Laurella's mum. "You're looking much better now, love," she observed. "And where did you find that gorgeous pendant?"

"It's literally just come into the shop," Joy answered quickly. "It really suits her doesn't it? It was definitely meant for her."

"Yes, it's really beautiful," admired Laurella's mum, lifting the pendant from her daughter's skin and gently rubbing her thumb over its surface. "Just

76

look at the amount of workmanship that's gone into carving it. It could be quite old you know."

If only you knew how old, thought Laurella to herself with the very slightest hint of a smirk. But then a rush of guilt rose in her body and made her face feel uncomfortably hot. She felt bad about not telling her mum and dad the truth but now really wasn't the time. She promised herself she would tell them everything very soon and she hoped they would believe her.

The sound of the till draw sliding shut shook Laurella out of her thoughts.

"Thanks again for everything Joy," said Laurella's dad as Joy handed over the faded old rug. She refused to take any payment for the pendant so he dropped a few pound coins in the collection box on the counter.

"Yes, thanks a lot Joy," added Laurella's mum, as the pensioner gave her and Laurella another enormous bear hug. "It's always great to see you and we'll definitely be back soon. And thanks again for keeping the rug to one side for us – who knows, it might even be a magic carpet!"

"You might just be right about that," laughed Joy, giving Laurella a knowing smile. I've always said this island is full of magic!"

Author's Note

~

I do hope you have enjoyed reading about Laurella's adventures in ancient Persia. I created Laurella so that my daughters could have a fictional hero who looked and acted just like them. I hope Laurella can be your hero too.

Although this story is made-up, some of it is loosely based on fact. Cyrus the Great was the founder of the Achaemenid Empire (pronounced Arkey-menid) and Pantea (pronounced Pan-tay-ah) and her husband General Aryasb (pronounced air-e-usb) were said to be commanders of the Immortals. I hope they did have a son like Artafarnah and, if he did have a pet, maybe it was a lion cub just like Zareen. Cyrus did have a palace in Pasargadae (pronounced pas-a-ga-day), but my palace description is based on the magnificent city of Persepolis which was built many years after his death (the ruins of which can still be seen today in Iran).

If you go online, you will be able to find lots of information about life in the Achaemenid Empire, including what people wore and what they ate. You can even go on a virtual tour of Persepolis at the height of its splendour. I've added some useful links over the next few pages to help get you started. I've also included a recipe for you to try so you can taste one of the dishes that Laurella sampled. And, you can have a go at writing in cuneiform script, just as Artafarnah would have done.

If you are lucky enough to visit the British Museum in London, you will see many items from ancient Persia, including the famous Cyrus Cylinder (a very important clay tablet that records information about Cyrus the Great and the way he ruled his empire). You will also see some of the intricate stone carvings, drinking vessels and jewellery mentioned in my story.

I don't know if Pantea ever owned a lioness pendant, but the one she gave to Laurella in my story is inspired by a real pendant that is housed in the Louvre museum in Paris.

Catford and Freshwater are real places in south London and the Isle of Wight, and they are well worth a visit. They both have great charity shops, packed with treasures. The old rug mentioned in my story is based on one I found locally.

I have a feeling that there are many more special keys in Joy's charity shop, just waiting to take Laurella on amazing adventures. So, the next time you're in a charity shop and see something of interest why don't you pause for a moment and try to imagine who could have owned it before and what amazing things might have happened in their lives?

~

Cook your own ancient Persian dish

~

Would you like a taste of ancient Persia? Follow this simple recipe and you can try roasted radishes, just like Laurella did. But remember to ask permission from an adult first.

Preparation time: 5 minutes
Cooking time: 15-20 minutes

Ingredients

- One pack of radishes (supermarkets usually sell them in 240g packs)
- One dessertspoon of olive oil (or vegetable oil, if you prefer)
- One level teaspoon of dried thyme
- One level teaspoon of dried rosemary
- A pinch of salt
- Black pepper to taste

Equipment

- Large bowl (big enough to fit all the radishes in)
- One baking tray lined with kitchen foil – or "Kee – chen – foi – al", as Artafarnah might say.
- One serving dish such as a dinner plate or cereal bowl (why not wrap your dish in kitchen foil and pretend that it's made of silver)
- A pair of scissors
- One dessertspoon
- One teaspoon
- Oven gloves
- Kitchen roll

Method

1) Preheat your oven to 180C or gas mark 6.

2) Wash the radishes then pat them dry with a piece of kitchen roll. If you like, you can use your scissors to snip off any roots or bits of green stem. Now place the radishes in a large bowl.

3) Drizzle the oil over the radishes and sprinkle on the thyme, rosemary, salt and pepper.

4) Mix everything up with your dessert spoon, ensuring your radishes have and even covering of oil, herbs, salt and pepper.

5) Tip the radishes into the baking tray and drizzle over any oil that's left in your bowl.

6) Using your oven gloves, place the radishes into your pre-heated oven and cook at 180C or gas mark 6 for 15-20 minutes. Give them a little shake every five minutes to make sure they cook evenly.

7) Using your oven gloves, remove the baking tray from the oven and place on a flat, heat-proof surface (a wooden chopping board would do just fine). Make sure you turn the oven off.

8) Carefully spoon your cooked radishes into your serving dish and enjoy hot or cold.

9) Please keep out of reach of hungry pets, especially cheeky lion cubs called Zareen.

Why don't you:
Keep one or two raw radishes to one side and do a taste comparison with your cooked ones. Which do you prefer?

You can find out more about what the Ancient Persians ate by visiting this webpage, but make sure you first get permission from an adult to use this link: Zoroastrian Heritage: Achaemenian Persian King's Table: *https://bit.ly/3h8dZ6f*

85

~

Have a go at writing in Ancient Persian script

~

The ancient Persians used a writing system called cuneiform, creating symbols by pressing a reed stylus into soft clay. The wedge-shaped impressions represented syllables or words.

I've tried to copy some of the symbols to see what Artafarnah, Laurella, Zareen and Allison would look like when written in Old Persian cuneiform.

Why don't you have a go too? Maybe you'd like to have a go at writing your name in Old Persian cuneiform? I've found an online cuneiform chart that can help you, but make sure you first get permission from an adult to use this link: http://www.iranchamber.com/scripts/old_persian_cuneiform.php

There's another cuneiform chart on this British Museum blog – and a video, showing you how to make your own cuneiform tablet with a lolly stick and some clay: *https://bit.ly/3hlEMfx*

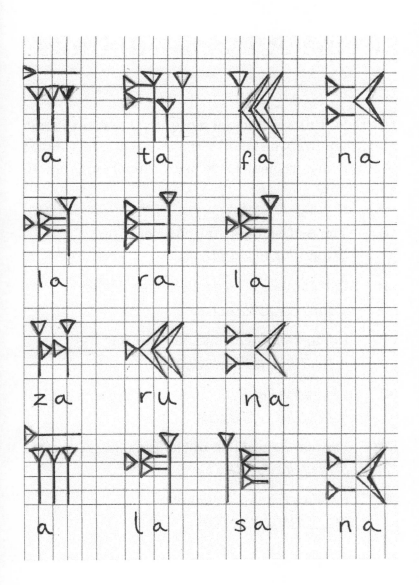

a	ta	fa	na
la	ra	la	
za	ru	na	
a	la	sa	na

87

~
Some other useful links
~

Use these links to find out more about ancient Persia and what life was like in the Achaemenid Empire – but always remember to ask permission from an adult first.

(1)   The British Museum - Ancient Iran
        https://bit.ly/3f0HILp

(2)   Persepolis – a virtual reconstruction
        https://bit.ly/3f2iTyY

(3)   Immortals (Achaemenid Empire)
        https://bit.ly/2QSm9Fb

(4)   Cyrus the Great
        https://bit.ly/2RySoc8

(5)   Pantea, Arteshbod of the Persian Immortals
        https://bit.ly/3tljKzS

(6)   Persian Lioness Pendant
        https://bit.ly/3w7hyyc

(7)   Human Rights and
        Rise of the Achaemenid Empire
        https://bit.ly/3et6h4W

(8)   Wikijunior: Ancient Civilizations/Persians
        https://bit.ly/3h5QSJh

(9)   Achaemenid Empire
        https://bit.ly/3tsd1nQ

(10)   Pasargadae
        https://bit.ly/3f6rZLc

(11)   Cyrus Cylinder
        https://bit.ly/2RBKNJR

(12)   Encyclopædia Iranica: Cassandane
        https://bit.ly/2QTsro0

~
Me and my stories
~

I thought you might want to know a little bit about me. Well, my name is Allison (with two ls) and I live in south London with my husband and our two daughters.

I've been a writer my whole working life, starting my career as a news reporter and then moving into communications, writing information for charities and businesses to help them tell people what they do. But recently I was drawn in a different direction – I began to write and illustrate children's stories.

I've written lots of stories (chapter books and picture books) but I'm still drawing the illustrations for some of them or reading through others and making a few final tweaks with a red pen! My stories can be about anything – haughty tigers, creepy clocks, magic carpets, mischievous babies, magical sea glass and, of course, a time-travelling 10-year-old called Laurella.

In fact, she started it all. She popped into my head one day a few years ago after my daughters (who are mixed race) complained about the lack of leading characters that look like them – especially in chapter books. I started to build a story around her and before I knew it, I found myself in ancient Persia! It was so much fun to write that I couldn't wait to send Laurella on another adventure and develop some of the other story ideas that came to me.

You can read an extract from my next Laurella Swift story over the next few pages and find out about the picture books I've published so far. By basing many of my characters and illustrations on my daughters, I hope to do my small bit to help more children see themselves in stories.

Just like Laurella's mum, I was born in Jersey (a beautiful little island in the English Channel). This probably explains my life-long obsession with the sea – and my overwhelming compulsion to pick up every shell, pebble or piece of sea glass that I come across whenever I'm at the seaside! I hope to share my love of the island with you in a new chapter book soon.

If you'd like to find out more about me and my books, ask an adult if you can visit my website: *www.tigerseyebooks.co.uk*

COMING SOON!

Are you ready for another adventure?
Read this extract from my next book:

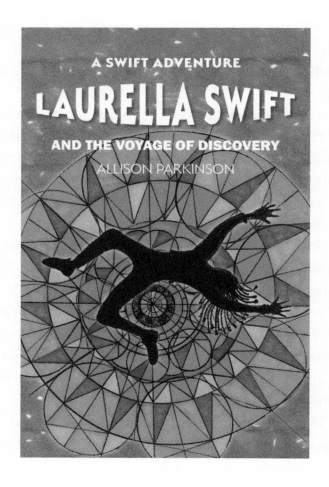

Laurella Swift and the Voyage of Discovery: Preview

Laurella looked up at the shop's gently ticking wall clock and made a mental note of the time. It was seven minutes past ten. Then she saw the rails and shelves of the charity shop slowly turn at right angles and suddenly splinter into a frieze of multi-coloured hexagons.

With every breath she took the shapes and colours changed again; now they were violet stars, crimson diamonds, turquoise triangles, amber circles and magenta hearts. All flowing in symmetry like living stained glass, each intricate pattern more exquisite and hypnotising than the last. Just as before, her body seemed to glide in effortless waves; up and down, up and down – a calming, rhythmic sensation like the roll and pull of the tide or the gentle inhale and exhale of breath. All traces of nausea had vanished and had now been replaced with an overwhelming sense of euphoria.

Gradually the waves subsided and Laurella became still. She watched passively as the shapes and colours around her gently melted back into her new surroundings. She slowly became aware of the rich, musty aroma of soil and damp wood, mixed with the sweet smell of new leaves – as crisp and fresh as the first bite of a green apple. An insect bussed close by her ear and, in the distance, she heard unfamiliar birdsong.

A cool breeze pricked her skin, and she opened her eyes into the opaque dawn light. She was standing in a small, almost perfect, heart-shaped clearing in a dense mature forest. Small ferns, heavy with dew, sprung up around her feet and at the edge of the clearing spectacular silver fronds of larger varieties gently nodded above her head. They reminded her of something – or somewhere – but try as she might, she couldn't quite pluck all the necessary information from her memory.

Frustrated, she pushed her way through the ferns and tugged on one of the many hanging creepers that crisscrossed the lower canopy like a giant game of cat's cradle. She stopped and craned her neck to follow the trunks of magnificent trees as they stretched up into the sky.

A faint fizzing sound like the crackle of static electricity popped and hissed near her left ear. She turned to see a solitary tree in amongst a clump of dense, evergreen bushes. It had thick glossy leaves, columns of cream blossom and, here and there, wrinkled clusters of orange berries. A small section of the trunk was glowing, just like the beads of the necklace in the charity shop.

So, this must be my key, Laurella deduced. *Some of the wood must have been used to make those tiny beads.*

At last, she remembered where she'd seen those large ferns before. They were in a dinosaur exhibition on the Isle of Wight. This sudden spark of memory gave her no comfort at all. Laurella began to scan the forest floor for any trace of reptilian tracks.

Twigs snapped and splintered, scaring birds from their lofty perches. Something was crashing through the undergrowth and heading straight towards Laurella. She dived into the heart of the largest bush and crouched in the dark green gloom, trying not to tremble. She held her breath and waited...

~

If you want to know what happens next, head to my website *www.tigerseyebooks.co.uk* for details on how you can get your hands on a copy of Laurella Swift and the Voyage of Discovery.

Tiger Tale

Zarif thinks that he is a very important and scary tiger but will a cat-loving lady feel the same? Find out what happens when the two meet in this rollicking rhyming story.

Children and adults won't be able to resist roaring along with the haughty hero in this fiendishly funny read-aloud picture book.

You can watch a video of me reading Tiger Tale at: *https://allisonparkinson.co.uk/my-books/tiger-tale/*

Tick-Tock

Layla doesn't like her Grandpa's new clock. She thinks it's creepy...but then she notices a teeny, tiny door. Find out what happens when she takes a closer look.

Learning to tell the time has never been so fun – or so noisy. With its expressive illustrations and rhythmic tone, this rhyming read-aloud picture book will keep young readers in suspense right up to the silly surprise ending. Humorous and heartfelt, this story celebrates diversity and the unique bond between grandparent and grandchild.

You can watch a video of me reading Tick-Tock at:
https://allisonparkinson.co.uk/my-books/tick-tock/

Write a review
~

I'd love to know what you and the adults in your life think of my books. If you'd like to leave a review on a site such as Toppsta or Goodreads you can find all the links in my blog: Write a review and share your love of reading at: *https://bit.ly/3cTDuoW*